Contents

Dogs at Work

People keep dogs for many different reasons.
Some dogs are kept to do jobs.
These dogs are called working dogs.

Dogs are born with very good **senses**.
They have an excellent sense of smell and good hearing.
Working dogs are taught to use their senses to do their jobs.

Working dogs can be different sizes and different **breeds**,
but they are all smart and keen to work.
They help people in many ways.

Working dogs help children and adults.

Farm Dogs

There are different kinds of farm dogs.
Herding dogs are good at herding,
or rounding up, other animals.
Herding dogs are trained to help move sheep, cows
and other animals safely from one place to another.
A herding dog does not hurt the animals.

A herding dog is taught to understand
the farmer's instructions.
The farmer uses words, whistles or hand signals
to tell the dog what to do.

Think and Talk About ...

Some farm dogs even herd ducks and chickens.

A farm dog herds sheep on a farm.

A large guard dog keeps watch over farm animals.

Some farm dogs work as guard dogs.
They are taught to protect
sheep, goats and other animals.
These guard dogs are large and strong
and do not get scared easily.
They protect the animals from **predators**,
such as wild dogs and wolves.

Think and Talk About ...

Guard dogs can work alone, or in pairs or teams.

Police Dogs

Police dogs are trained to help the police to do their job.
Each dog works with a police officer.
They work during the day and at night.

Police dogs are fit and strong.
They use their excellent sense of smell
to find people, animals, plants and objects.

Police dogs also protect people and **property**.

A police dog follows a scent to help find something.

Police dogs work in many different places, such as on the streets and at airports. Sometimes, the dogs have to go into small spaces, such as inside sheds and cars.

Police dogs are taught to be calm in a crowd. They cannot be scared of loud noises.

Working with a police officer can be dangerous, so police dogs sometimes wear special vests that help to protect their bodies.

Think and Talk About ...

A police dog works with one police officer. Sometimes, the dog even lives with the officer.

This dog is checking bags at the airport.

Search and Rescue Dogs

Search and rescue dogs are used to search for lost or trapped people. Each dog works with a trainer. The dogs use their strong sense of smell to find people.

Sometimes, the dogs search for people who are lost in places like forests.

Sometimes, the dogs find people who are trapped under dirt or snow. They also find people who are trapped inside fallen buildings.

A search and rescue dog has to work quickly to chase a scent.

A search and rescue dog helps after an earthquake.

Search and rescue dogs and their trainers
often work in dangerous places,
such as areas that have been hit by earthquakes.

Search and rescue dogs are fit and strong.
Sometimes, the dogs must work
for many hours in very hot or cold weather.

Think and Talk About ...

Trainers work with search and rescue dogs every week, so the dogs are always ready to help.

Guide Dogs

Guide dogs help people who are **blind** to move about safely.
A guide dog wears a harness.
The person who is blind holds on to a handle on the harness.
When the dog and person walk together,
the dog guides the person safely around objects.

A guide dog can lead a person across the road,
into shops, onto a train and to many other places.

Think and Talk About ...

In countries around the world, guide dogs help people who are blind.

A person who is blind is led across a road by her guide dog.

It takes many months to train a guide dog.
Training usually starts when the dog is about one year old.

Once the training is finished, the dog goes to a person who is blind.
They learn to work together
and the guide dog lives with the person who is blind.

Most guide dogs work for about eight to ten years.

A guide dog trainer uses hand signals to train this puppy.

Once a guide dog has been trained, it lives at the home of a person who is blind.

Sled Dogs

Sled dogs are taught to pull sleds over snow and ice.
The dogs have thick fur, so they can live in cold places.
They are strong and can run for a long time.
These dogs have a lot of **energy**.

Sled dogs usually work in a team, with a person as the driver.
Each dog wears a harness to help pull the sled.
The dogs often wear special socks, called booties.
The booties protect the dogs' paws.

Sled dogs pull a sled across snow.

Dogs That Act

Some dogs even work in movies, or in television shows. They sometimes appear in photographs for goods, such as dog food.

Acting dogs are taught to do tricks. Some tricks are difficult. Dogs that act can be any breed and any size. They work with people, other animals and objects.

This acting dog even performs on the red carpet!

Working dogs do lots of different jobs. They use their strong senses to help people in many ways. Working dogs are great to have around because they help keep people and other animals safe.

Glossary

blind (*adjective*) not being able to see well, or at all

breeds (*noun*) different kinds of dogs

energy (*noun*) the power to move and to work

predators (*noun*) animals that eat other animals

property (*noun*) a piece of land, a building or an object that belongs to someone

senses (*noun*) hearing, seeing, smell, taste and touch

Index